THE ASSASSINS

BY

PERCY BYSSHE SHELLEY

British Library Cataloguing-in-Publication Data
A catalogue record for this book is available from the
British Library

CONTENTS

PERCY BYSSHE SHELLEY

Percy Bysshe Shelley was born in Horsham, Sussex, England in 1792. He studied at University College, Oxford, but his atheistic views got him expelled. Estranged from his father, he left home and began to take trips to London to spend time with famous journalist William Godwin. It was here, around the time that he published *Queen Mab: A Philosophical Poem* (1813), that Shelley met the Godwin's daughter, Mary, quickly striking up a romantic relationship with her. In 1814, the two of them eloped to Switzerland, where they spent time with Lord Byron, and where the young Mary Shelley found the inspiration for her future masterpiece, *Frankenstein* (1818).

In 1815, the Shelleys moved back to London, where the two of them continued to write. Percy was a prolific producer of literature, and many of the verse works he penned in the last seven or eight years of his life — such as *Ozymandias, Ode to the West Wind, To a Skylark, Music, When Soft Voices Die, The Cloud* and *The Masque of Anarchy* — are now considered some of the best in the English language. He was also known for his uncompromising idealism, most notably as a fierce advocate of non-violence and vegetarianism. Shelley spent the latter part of life in Italy, where he drowned during a

1

sailing trip in 1822, aged just 29. It wasn't until after his passing that he developed a large following, and since his death writers as varied as George Bernard Shaw, Bertrand Russell and Karl Marx have all expressed their admiration for him.

THE ASSASSINS

Percy Bysshe Shelley

I

JERUSALEM, goaded to resistance by the incessant usurpations and insolence of Rome, leagued together its discordant factions to rebel against the common enemy and tyrant. Inferior to their foe in all but the unconquerable hope of liberty, they surrounded their city with fortifications of uncommon strength, and placed in array before the temple a band rendered desperate by patriotism and religion. Even the women preferred to die, rather than survive the ruin of their country. When the Roman army approached the walls of the sacred city, its preparations, its discipline, and its numbers, evinced the conviction of its leader, that he had no common barbarians to subdue. At the approach of the Roman army, the strangers withdrew from the city.

Among the multitudes which from every nation of the East had assembled at Jerusalem, was a little congregation of Christians. They were remarkable neither for their numbers nor their importance. They contained among them neither philosophers nor poets. Acknowledging no laws but those of God, they modelled their conduct towards their fellowmen by the conclusions of their individual judgment on the practical application of these laws. And it was apparent from the simplicity and severity of their manners, that this contempt for human institutions had produced among them a character superior in singleness and sincere self-apprehension to the slavery of pagan customs and the gross delusions of antiquated superstition. Many of their opinions considerably resembled those of the sect afterwards known by the name of Gnostics. They esteemed the human understanding to be the paramount rule of human conduct; they maintained that the obscurest religious truth required for its complete elucidation no more than the strenuous application of the energies of mind. It appeared impossible to them that any doctrine could be subversive of social happiness which is not capable of being confuted by arguments derived from the nature of existing things. With the devoutest submission to the law of Christ, they united an intrepid spirit of inquiry as to the correctest mode of acting in particular instances of conduct that occur among men. Assuming the doctrines of the Messiah concerning benevolence and justice for the regulation of their actions, they could not be persuaded to acknowledge that there was apparent in the divine code any prescribed rule whereby, for its own sake, one action rather than another, as fulfilling the will of their great Master, should be preferred.

The contempt with which the magistracy and priesthood regarded this obscure community of speculators, had hitherto protected them from persecution. But they had arrived at that precise degree of eminence and prosperity which is peculiarly obnoxious to the hostility of the rich and powerful. The moment of their departure from Jerusalem was the crisis of their future destiny. Had they continued to seek a precarious refuge in a city of the Roman empire, this persecution would not have delayed to impress a new character on their opinions and their conduct; narrow views, and the illiberality of sectarian patriotism, would not have failed speedily to obliterate the magnificence and beauty of their wild and wonderful condition.

Attached from principle to peace, despising and hating the pleasures and the customs of the degenerate mass of mankind, this unostentatious community of good and happy men fled to the solitudes of Lebanon. To Arabians and enthusiasts the solemnity and grandeur of these desolate recesses possessed peculiar attractions. It well accorded with the justice of their conceptions on the relative duties of man towards his fellow in society, that they should labour in unconstrained equality to dispossess the wolf and the tiger of their empire, and establish on its ruins the dominion of intelligence and virtue. No longer would the worshippers of the God of Nature be indebted to a hundred hands for the accommodation of their simple wants. No longer would the poison of a diseased civilization embrue their very nutriment with pestilence. They would no longer owe their very existence to the vices, the fears, and the follies of mankind. Love, friendship, and philanthropy, would now be the characteristic disposers of their industry. It is for his mistress or his friend that the labourer consecrates his toil; others are mindful, but he is forgetful, of himself. 'God feeds the hungry ravens, and clothes the lilies of the fields, and yet Solomon in all his glory is not like to one of these.'

Rome was now the shadow of her former self. The light of her grandeur and loveliness had passed away. The latest and the noblest of her poets and historians had foretold in agony her approaching slavery and degradation. The ruins of the human mind, more awful and portentous than the desolation of the most solemn temples, threw a shade of gloom upon her golden palaces which the brutal vulgar could not see, but which the mighty felt with inward trepidation and despair. The ruins of Jerusalem lay defenceless and uninhabited upon the burning sands; one visited, but in the depth of solemn awe, this accursed and solitary spot. Tradition says that there was seen to linger among the scorched and shattered fragments of the temple, one being, whom he that saw dared not to call man, with clasped hands, immoveable eyes, and a visage horribly serene. Not on the will of the capricious multitude, nor the constant fluctuations of the many and the weak, depends the change of empires and religions. These are the mere insensible elements from which a subtler intelligence moulds its enduring statuary. They that direct the changes of this mortal scene breathe the decrees of their dominion from a throne of darkness and of tempest. The power of man is great.

After many days of wandering, the Assassins pitched their tents in the valley of Bethzatanai. For ages had this fertile valley lain concealed from the adventurous search of man, among mountains of everlasting snow. The men of elder days had inhabited this spot. Piles of monumental marble and fragments of columns that in their integrity almost seemed the work of some intelligence more sportive and fantastic than the gross conceptions of mortality, lay in heaps beside the lake, and were visible beneath its transparent waves. The flowering orange-tree, the balsam, and innumerable odiferous shrubs, grew wild in the desolated portals. The fountain tanks had overflowed; and, amid the luxuriant vegetation of their margin the yellow snake held its unmolested dwelling. Hither came the tiger and the bear to contend for those once domestic animals who had forgotten the secure servitude of their ancestors. No sound, when the famished beast of prey had retreated in despair from the awful desolation of this place, at whose completion he had assisted, but the shrill cry of the stork, and the flapping of his heavy wings from the capital of the solitary column, and the scream of the hungry vulture baffled of its only victim. The lore of ancient wisdom sculptured in mystic characters on the rocks. The human spirit and the human hand had been busy here to accomplish its profoundest miracles. It was a temple dedicated to the God of knowledge and of truth. The palaces of the Caliphs and the Caesars might easily surpass these ruins in magnitude and sumptuousness: but they were the designs of tyrants and the work of slaves. Piercing genius and consummate prudence had planned and executed Bethzatanai. There was deep and important meaning in every lineament of its fantastic sculpture. The unintelligible legend, once so beautiful and perfect, so full of poetry and history, spoke, even in destruction, volumes of mysterious import, and obscure significance.

But in the season of its utmost prosperity and magnificence, art might not aspire to vie with nature in the valley of Bethzatanai. All that was wonderful and lovely was collected in this deep seclusion. The fluctuating elements seemed to have been rendered everlastingly permanent in forms of wonder and delight. The mountains of Lebanon had been divided to their base to form this happy valley; on every side their icy summits darted their white pinnacles into the clear blue sky, imaging, in their grotesque outline, minarets, and ruined domes, and columns worn with time. Far below, the silver clouds rolled their bright volumes in many beautiful shapes, and fed the eternal springs that, spanning the dark chasms like a thousand radiant rainbows, leaped into the quiet vale, then, lingering in many a dark glade among the groves of cypress and of palm, lost themselves in the lake. The immensity of these precipitous mountains, with their starry pyramids of snow, excluded the sun, which overtopped not, even in its meridian, their overhanging rocks. But a more heavenly and serener light was reflected from their icy mirrors, which, piercing through the many-tinted clouds, produced lights and colours of inexhaustible variety. The herbage was perpetually verdant, and clothed the darkest recesses of the caverns and the woods.

Nature, undisturbed, had become an enchantress in these solitudes: she had collected here all that was wonderful and divine from the armoury of her omnipotence. The very winds breathed health and renovation, and the joyousness of youthful courage. Fountains of crystalline water played perpetually among the aromatic flowers, and mingled a freshness with their odour. The pine boughs became instruments of exquisite contrivance, among which every varying breeze waked music of new and more delightful melody. Meteoric shapes, more effulgent than the moonlight, hung on the wandering clouds, and mixed in discordant dance around the spiral fountains. Blue vapours assume strange lineaments under the rocks and among the ruins, lingering like ghosts with slow and solemn step. Through a dark chasm to the east, in the long perspective of a portal glittering with the unnumbered riches of the subterranean world, shone the broad moon, pouring in one yellow and unbroken stream her horizontal beams. Nearer the icy region, autumn and spring held an alternate reign. The sere leaves fell and choked the sluggish brooks; the chilling fogs hung diamonds on every spray; and in the dark cold evening the howling winds made melancholy music in the trees. Far above, shone the bright throne of winter, clear, cold, and dazzling. Sometimes there was seen the snowflakes to fall before the sinking orb of the beamless sun, like a shower of fiery sulphur. The cataracts, arrested in their course, seemed, with their transparent columns, to support the darkbrowed rocks. Sometimes the icy whirlwind scooped the powdery snow aloft, to mingle with the hissing meteors, and scatter spangles through the rare and rayless atmosphere.

Such strange scenes of chaotic confusion and harrowing sublimity, surrounding and shutting in the vale, added to the delights of its secure and voluptuous tranquillity. No spectator could have refused to believe that some spirit of great intelligence and power had hallowed these wild and beautiful solitudes to a deep and solemn mystery.

The immediate effect of such a scene, suddenly presented to the contemplation of mortal eyes, is seldom the subject of authentic record. The coldest slave of custom cannot fail to recollect some few moments in which the breath of spring or the crowding clouds of sunset, with the pale moon shining through their fleecy skirts, or the song of some lonely bird perched on the only tree of an unfrequented heath, has awakened the touch of nature. And they were Arabians who entered the valley of Bethzatanai; men who idolated nature and the God of nature; to whom love and lofty thoughts, and the apprehensions of an uncorrupted spirit, were sustenance and life. Thus securely excluded from an abhorred world, all thought of its judgment was cancelled by the rapidity of their fervid imaginations. They ceased to acknowledge, or deigned not to advert to, the distinctions with which the majority of base and vulgar minds control the longings and struggles of the soul towards its place of rest. A new and sacred fire was kindled in their hearts and sparkled in their eyes. Every gesture, every feature, the minutest action, was modelled to beneficence and beauty by the holy inspiration that had descended on their searching spirits. The epidemic transport communicated itself through every heart with the rapidity of a blast from heaven. They were already disembodied spirits; they were already the inhabitants of paradise. To live, to breathe, to move, was itself a sensation of immeasurable transport. Every new contemplation of the condition of his nature brought to the happy enthusiast an added measure of delight, and impelled to every organ, where mind is united with external things, a keener and more exquisite perception of all that they contain of lovely and divine. To love, to be beloved, suddenly became an insatiable famine of his nature, which the wide circle of the universe, comprehending beings of such inexhaustible variety and stupendous magnitude of excellence, appeared too narrow and confined to satiate.

Alas, that these visitings of the spirit of life should fluctuate and pass away! That the moments when the human mind is commensurate with all that it can conceive of excellent and powerful, should not endure with its existence and survive its most momentous change! But the beauty of a vernal sunset with its overhanging curtains of empurpled cloud, is rapidly dissolved, to return at some unexpected period, and spread an alleviating melancholy over the dark vigils of despair.

It is true the enthusiasm of overwhelming transport which had inspired every breast among the Assassins is no more. The necessity of daily occupation and the ordinariness of that human life, the burthen of which it is the destiny of every human being to bear, had smothered, not extinguished, that divine and eternal fire. Not the less indelible and permanent were the impressions communicated to all; not the more unalterably were the features of their social character modelled and determined by its influence.

II

Rome had fallen. Her senate-house had become a polluted den of thieves and liars; her solemn temples, the arena of theological disputants, who made fire and sword the missionaries of their inconceivable beliefs. The city of the monster Constantine, symbolizing, in the consequences of its foundation, the wickedness and weakness of his successors, feebly imagined with declining power the substantial eminence of the Roman name. Pilgrims of a new and mightier faith crowded to visit the lonely ruins of Jerusalem, and weep and pray before the sepulchre of the Eternal God. The earth was filled with discord, tumult, and ruin. The spirit of disinterested virtue had armed one-half of the civilized world against the other. Monstrous and detestable creeds poisoned and blighted the domestic charities. There was no appeal to natural love, or ancient faith, from pride, superstition, and revenge.

Four centuries had passed thus, terribly characterized by the most calamitous revolutions. The Assassins, meanwhile, undisturbed by the surrounding tumult, possessed and cultivated their fertile valley. The gradual operation of their peculiar condition had matured and perfected the singularity and excellence of their character. That cause, which had ceased to act as an immediate and overpowering excitement, became the unperceived law of their lives, and sustenance of their natures. Their religious tenets had also undergone a change, corresponding with the exalted condition of their moral being. The gratitude which they owed to the benignant Spirit by which their limited intelligences had not only been created but redeemed, was less frequently adverted to, became less the topic of comment or contemplation; not, therefore, did it cease to be their presiding guardian, the guide of their inmost thoughts, the tribunal of appeal for the minutest particulars of their conduct. They learned to identify this mysterious benefactor with the delight that is bred among the solitary rocks, and has its dwelling alike in the changing colours of the clouds and the inmost recesses of the caverns. Their future also no longer existed, but in the blissful tranquillity of the present. Time was measured and created by the vices and the miseries of men, between whom and the happy nation of the Assassins, there was no analogy nor comparison. Already had their eternal peace commenced. The darkness had passed away from the open gates of death.

The practical results produced by their faith and condition upon their external conduct were singular and memorable. Excluded from the great and various community of mankind, these solitudes became to them a sacred hermitage, in which all formed, as it were, one being, divided against itself by no contending will or factious passions. Every impulse conspired to one end, and tended to a single object. Each devoted his powers to the happiness of the other. Their republic was the scene of the perpetual contentions of benevolence; not the heartless and assumed kindness of commercial man, but the genuine virtue that has a legible superscription in every feature of the countenance, and every motion of the frame. The perverseness and calamities of those who dwelt beyond the mountains that encircled their undisturbed possessions, were unknown and unimagined. Little embarrassed by the complexities of civilized society, they knew not to conceive any happiness that can be satiated without participation, or that thirsts not to reproduce and perpetually generate itself. The path of virtue and felicity was plain and unimpeded. They clearly acknowledged, in every case, that conduct to be entitled to preference which would obviously produce the greatest pleasure. They could not conceive an instance in which it would be their duty to hesitate, in causing, at whatever expense, the greatest and most unmixed delight.

Hence arose a peculiarity which only failed to germinate in uncommon and momentous consequences, because the Assassins had retired from the intercourse of mankind, over whom other motives and principles of conduct than justice and benevolence prevail. It would be a difficult matter for men of such a sincere and simple faith, to estimate the final results of their intentions, among the corrupt and slavish multitude. They would be perplexed also in their choice of the means, whereby their intentions might be fulfilled. To produce immediate pain or disorder for the sake of future benefit, is consonant, indeed, with the purest religion and philosophy, but never fails to excite invincible repugnance in the feelings of the many. Against their predilections and distastes an Assassin, accidentally the inhabitant of a civilized community, would wage unremitting hostility from principle. He would find himself compelled to adopt means which they would abhor, for the sake of an object which they could not conceive that he should propose to himself. Secure and self-enshrined in the magnificence and pre-eminence of his conceptions, spotless as the light of heaven, he would be the victim among men of calumny and persecution. Incapable of distinguishing his motives, they would rank him among the vilest and most atrocious criminals. Great, beyond all comparison with them, they would despise him in the presumption of their ignorance. Because his spirit burned with an unquenchable passion for their welfare, they would lead him, like his illustrious master, amidst scoffs, and mockery, and insult, to the remuneration of an ignominious death.

Who hesitates to destroy a venomous serpent that has crept near his sleeping friend, except the man who selfishly dreads lest the malignant reptile should turn his fury on himself? And if the poisoner has assumed a human shape, if the bane be distinguished only from the viper's venom by the excess and extent of its devastation, will the saviour and avenger here retract and pause entrenched behind the superstition of the indefeasible divinity of man? Is the human form, then, the mere badge of a prerogative for unlicensed wickedness and mischief? Can the power derived from the weakness of the oppressed, or the ignorance of the deceived, confer the right in security to tyrannize and defraud?

The subject of regular governments, and the disciple of established superstition, dares not ask this question. For the sake of the eventual benefit, he endures what he esteems a transitory evil, and the moral degradation of man disquiets not his patience. But the religion of an Assassin imposes other virtues than endurance, when his fellow-men groan under tyranny, or have become so bestial and abject that they cannot feel their chains. An Assassin believes that man is eminently man, and only then enjoys the prerogatives of his privileged condition, when his affections and his judgment pay tribute to the God of Nature. The perverse, and vile, and vicious — what were they? Shapes of some unholy vision, moulded by the spirit of Evil, which the sword of the merciful destroyer should sweep from this beautiful world. Dreamy nothings; phantasms of misery and mischief, that hold their death-like state on glittering thrones, and in the loathsome dens of poverty. No Assassin would submissively temporize with vice, and in cold charity become a pander to falsehood and desolation. His path through the wilderness of civilized society would be marked with the blood of the oppressor and the ruiner. The wretch, whom nations tremblingly adore, would expiate in his throttling grasp a thousand licensed and venerable crimes.

How many holy liars and parasites, in solemn guise, would his saviour arm drag from their luxurious couches, and plunge in the cold charnel, that the green and many-legged monsters of the slimy grave might eat off at their leisure the lineaments of rooted malignity and detested cunning. The respectable man — the smooth, smiling, polished villain, whom all the city honours; whose very trade is lies and murder; who buys his daily bread with the blood and tears of men, would feed the ravens with his limbs. The Assassin would cater nobly for the eyeless worms of earth, and the carrion fowls of heaven.

Yet here, religion and human love had imbued the manners of those solitary people with inexpressible gentleness and benignity. Courage and active virtue, and the indignation against vice, which becomes a hurrying and irresistible passion, slept like the imprisoned earthquake, or the lightning shafts that hang in the golden clouds of evening. They were innocent, but they were capable of more than innocence; for the great principles of their faith were perpetually acknowledged and adverted to; nor had they forgotten, in this uninterrupted quiet, the author of their felicity.

Four centuries had thus worn away without producing an event. Men had died, and natural tears had been shed upon their graves, in sorrow that improves the heart. Those who had been united by love had gone to death together, leaving to their friends the bequest of a most sacred grief, and of a sadness that is allied to pleasure. Babes that hung upon their mothers' breasts had become men; men had died; and many a wild luxuriant weed that overtopped the habitations of the vale, had twined its roots around their disregarded bones. Their tranquil state was like a summer sea, whose gentle undulations disturb not the reflected stars, and break not the long still line of the rainbow hues of sunrise.

III

Where all is thus calm, the slightest circumstance is recorded and remembered. Before the sixth century had expired one incident occurred, remarkable and strange. A young man, named Albedir, wandering in the woods, was startled by the screaming of a bird of prey, and, looking up, saw blood fall, drop by drop, from among the intertwined boughs of a cedar. Having climbed the tree, he beheld a terrible and dismaying spectacle. A naked human body was impaled on the broken branch. It was maimed and mangled horribly; every limb bent and bruised into frightful distortion, and exhibiting a breathing image of the most sickening mockery of life. A monstrous snake had scented its prey from among the mountains — and above hovered a hungry vulture. From amidst this mass of desolated humanity, two eyes, black and inexpressibly brilliant, shone with an unearthly lustre. Beneath the blood-stained eye-brows their steady rays manifested the serenity of an immortal power, the collected energy of a deathless mind, spell-secured from dissolution. A bitter smile of mingled abhorrence and scorn distorted his wounded lip — he appeared calmly to observe and measure all around — self-possession had not deserted the shattered mass of life.

The youth approached the bough on which the breathing corpse was hung. As he approached, the serpent reluctantly un-wreathed his glittering coils, and crept towards his dark and loathsome cave. The vulture, impatient of his meal, fled to the mountain, that re-echoed with his hoarse screams. The cedar branches creaked with their agitating weight, faintly, as the dismal wind arose. All else was deadly silent.

At length a voice issued from the mangled man. It rattled in hoarse murmurs from his throat and lungs — his words were the conclusion of some strange mysterious soliloquy. They were broken, and without apparent connection, completing wide intervals of inexpressible conceptions.

'The great tyrant is baffled, even in success. Joy! joy! to his tortured foe! Triumph to the worm whom he tramples under his feet! Ha! His suicidal hand might dare as well abolish the mighty frame of things! Delight and exultation sit before the closed fates of death! — I fear not to dwell beneath their black and ghastly shadow. Here thy power may not avail! Thou createst — 'tis mine to ruin and destroy. — I was thy slave — I am thy equal, and thy foe. — Thousands tremble before thy throne, who, at my voice, shall dare to pluck the golden crown from thine unholy head!' He ceased. The silence of noon swallowed up his words. Albedir clung tighter to the tree — he dared not for dismay remove his eyes. He remained mute in the perturbation of deep and creeping horror.

'Albedir!' said the same voice, 'Albedir! in the name of God, approach. He that suffered me to fall, watches thee; — the gentle and merciful spirits of sweet human love, delight not in agony and horror. For pity's sake approach, in the name of thy good God, approach, Albedir!' The tones were mild and clear as the responses of Aeolian music. They floated to Albedir's ear like the warm breath of June that lingers in the lawny groves, subduing all to softness. Tears of tender affection started into his eyes. It was as the voice of a beloved friend. The partner of his childhood, the brother of his soul, seemed to call for aid, and pathetically to remonstrate with delay. He resisted not the magic impulse, but advanced towards the spot, and tenderly attempted to remove the wounded man. He cautiously descended the tree with his wretched burthen, and deposited it on the ground.

A period of strange silence intervened. Awe and cold horror were slowly proceeding to the softer sensations of tumultuous pity, when again he heard the silver modulations of the same enchanting voice. 'Weep not for me, Albedir! What wretch so utterly lost, but might inhale peace and renovation from this paradise! I am wounded, and in pain; but having found a refuge in this seclusion, and a friend in you, I am worthier of envy than compassion. Bear me to your cottage secretly: I would not disturb your gentle partner by my appearance.

She must love me more dearly than a brother. I must be the playmate of your children; already I regard them with a father's love. My arrival must not be regarded as a thing of mystery and wonder. What, indeed, but that men are prone to error and exaggeration, is less inexplicable, than that a stranger, wandering on Lebanon, fell from the rocks into the vale? Albedir,' he continued, and his deepening voice assumed awful solemnity, 'in return for the affection with which I cherish thee and thine, thou owest this submission.'

Albedir implicitly submitted; not even a thought had power to refuse its deference. He reassumed his burthen, and proceeded towards the cottage. He watched until Khaled should be absent, and conveyed the stranger into an apartment appropriated for the reception of those who occasionally visited their habitation. He desired that the door should be securely fastened, and that he might not be visited until the morning of the following day.

Albedir waited with impatience for the return of Khaled. The unaccustomed weight of even so transitory a secret, hung on his ingenuous and unpractised nature, like a blighting, clinging curse. The stranger's accents had lulled him to a trance of wild and delightful imagination. Hopes, so visionary and aerial, that they had assumed no denomination, had spread themselves over his intellectual frame, and, phantoms as they were, had modelled his being to their shape. Still his mind was not exempt from the visitings of disquietude and perturbation. It was a troubled stream of thought, over whose fluctuating waves un-searchable fate seemed to preside, guiding its unforeseen alternations with an inexorable hand. Albedir paced earnestly the garden of his cottage, revolving every circumstance attendant on the incident of the day. He re-imaged with intense thought the minutest recollections of the scene. In vain — he was the slave of suggestions not to be controlled. Astonishment, horror, and awe — tumultuous sympathy, and a mysterious elevation of soul, hurried away all activity of judgment, and overwhelmed, with stunning force, every attempt at deliberation or inquiry.

His reveries were interrupted at length by the return of Khaled. She entered the cottage, that scene of undisturbed repose, in the confidence that change might as soon overwhelm the eternal world, as disturb this inviolable sanctuary. She started to behold Albedir. Without preface or remark, he recounted with eager haste the occurrences of the day. Khaled's tranquil spirit could hardly keep pace with the breathless rapidity of his narration. She was bewildered with staggering wonder even to hear his confused tones, and behold his agitated countenance.

IV

On the following morning Albedir arose at sunrise, and visited the stranger. He found him already risen, and employed in adorning the lattice of his chamber with flowers from the garden. There was something in his attitude and occupation singularly expressive of his entire familiarity with the scene. Albedir's habitation seemed to have been his accustomed home. He addressed his host in a tone of gay and affectionate welcome, such as never fails to communicate by sympathy the feelings from which it flows.

'My friend,' said he, 'the balm of the dew of our vale is sweet; or is this garden the favoured spot where the winds conspire to scatter the best odours they can find? Come, lend me your arm awhile, I feel very weak.' He motioned to walk forth, but, as if unable to proceed, rested on the seat beside the door. For a few moments they were silent, if the interchange of cheerful and happy looks is to be called silence. At last he observed a spade that rested against the wall. 'You have only one spade, brother,' said he; 'you have only one, I suppose, of any of the instruments of tillage. Your garden ground, too, occupies a certain space which it will be necessary to enlarge. This must be quickly remedied. I cannot earn my supper of tonight, nor of tomorrow; but thenceforward, I do not mean to eat the bread of idleness. I know that you would willingly perform the additional labour which my nourishment would require; I know, also, that you would feel a degree of pleasure in the fatigue arising from this employment, but I shall contest with you such pleasures as these, and such pleasures as these alone.' His eyes were somewhat wan, and the tone of his voice languid as he spoke.

As they were thus engaged, Khaled came towards them. The stranger beckoned to her to sit beside him, and taking her hands within his own, looked attentively on her mild countenance. Khaled inquired if he had been refreshed by sleep. He replied by a laugh of careless and inoffensive glee; and placing one of her hands within Albedir's, said, 'If this be sleep, here in this odorous vale, where these sweet smiles encompass us, and the voices of those who love are heard — if these be the visions of sleep, sister, those who lie down in misery shall arise lighter than the butterflies. I came from amid the tumult of a world, how different from this! I am unexpectedly among you, in the midst of a scene such as my imagination never dared to promise. I must remain here — I must not depart.' Khaled, recovering from the admiration and astonishment caused by the stranger's words and manner, assured him of the happiness which she should feel in such an addition to her society. Albedir, too, who had been more deeply impressed than Khaled by the event of his arrival, earnestly re-assured him of the ardour of the affection with which he had inspired them. The stranger smiled gently to hear the unaccustomed fervour of sincerity which animated their address, and was rising to retire, when Khaled said, 'You have not yet seen our children, Maimuna and Abdallah. They are by the water-side, playing with their favourite snake. We have only to cross yonder little wood, and wind down a patch cut in the rock that overhangs the lake, and we shall find them, beside a recess which the shore makes there, and which a chasm, as it were the rocks and woods, encloses. Do you think you could walk there?' — 'To see your children, Khaled? I think I could, with the assistance of Albedir's arm, and yours.' — So they went through the wood of ancient cypress, intermingled with the brightness of many-tinted blooms, which gleamed like stars through its romantic glens. They crossed the green meadow, and entered among the broken chasms, beautiful as they were in their investiture of odiferous shrubs. They came at last, after pursuing a path which wound though the intricacies of a little wilderness, to the borders of the lake. They stood on the rock which overhung it, from which there was a prospect of all the miracles of nature and of art which encircled and adorned its shores. The stranger gazed upon it with a countenance unchanged by any emotion, but, as it were, thoughtfully and contemplatingly. As he gazed, Khaled ardently pressed his hand, and said, in a low yet eager voice, 'Look, look, lo there!' He turned towards her, but her eyes were not on him. She looked below — her lips were parted by the feelings which possessed her soul — her breath came and went regularly but inaudibly. She leaned over the precipice, and her dark hair hanging beside her face, gave relief to its fine lineaments, animated by such love as exceeds utterance. The stranger followed her eyes, and saw that her children were in the glen below; then raising his eyes, exchanged with her affectionate looks of congratulation and delight. The boy was apparently eight years old, the girl about two years younger. The beauty of their form and countenance was something so divine and strange, as overwhelmed the senses of the beholder like a delightful dream, with insupportable ravishment. They were arrayed in a loose robe of linen, through which the exquisite proportions of their form appeared. Unconscious that they were observed, they did not relinquish the occupation in which they were engaged. They had constructed a little boat of the bark of trees, and had given it sails of interwoven feathers, and launched it on the water. They sat beside a white flat stone, on which a small snake lay coiled, and when their work was finished, they arose and called to the snake in melodious tones, so that it understood their language. For it unwreathed its shining circles and crept to the boat, into which no sooner had it entered, than the girl loosened the band which held it to the shore, and it sailed away. Then they ran round and round the little creek, clapping their hands, and melodiously pouring out wild sounds, which the snake seemed to answer by the restless glancing of his neck. At last a breath of wind came from the shore, and the boat changed its course, and was about to leave the creek, which the snake perceived and leaped into the water, and came to the little children's feet. The girl sang to it, and it leaped into her bosom, and she crossed her fair hands over it, as if to cherish it there. Then the boy answered with a song, and it glided from beneath her hands and crept towards him. While they were thus employed, Maimuna looked up, and seeing her parents on the cliff, ran to meet them up the steep path that wound round it; and Abdallah, leaving his snake, followed joyfully.

www.ingramcontent.com/pod-product-compliance
Lightning Source LLC
Chambersburg PA
CBHW030531260626
47157CB00005B/1985